D0409434

Peter Rabbit™ Tales
Beatrix Potter

She looked suspiciously at the sack and wondered where everybody was?

PETER RABBIT™
TALES

THE ORIGINAL AND AUTHORIZED EDITION BY

BEATRIX POTTER

New colour reproductions

FREDERICK WARNE

The reproductions in this book have been made using the most modern electronic scanning methods from entirely new transparencies of Beatrix Potter's original watercolours. They enable Beatrix Potter's skill as an artist to be appreciated as never before, not even during her own lifetime.

FREDERICK WARNE
Published by the Penguin Group
Penguin Books Ltd, 27 Wrights Lane, London W8 5TZ, England
Penguin Putnam Inc., 375 Hudson Street, New York, NY 10014, USA
Penguin Books Australia Ltd, Ringwood, Victoria, Australia
Penguin Books Canada Ltd, 10 Alcorn Avenue, Toronto, Ontario, Canada M4V 3B2
Penguin Books (N.Z.) Ltd, 182-190 Wairau Road, Auckland 10, New Zealand

Penguin Books Ltd, Registered Offices: Harmondsworth, Middlesex, England

First published in 1998 by Frederick Warne

1 3 5 7 9 10 8 6 4 2

ISBN 0 7232 4483 9

Printed and bound in Great Britain by William Clowes Limited, Beccles and London

CONTENTS

THE STORY OF BEATRIX POTTER

Beatrix, aged 8, with her parents, Rupert and Helen Potter

Beatrix Potter was born in 1866 to Rupert and Helen Potter. She had a conventionally sheltered Victorian childhood and was educated at home by a governess. Beatrix's well-to-do parents disapproved of her forming friendships with children of her own age, so she had a somewhat lonely childhood. Though she was not allowed to mix with her peers, Beatrix met many famous artists, politicians and thinkers when they came to visit her father. For companionship, Beatrix and her younger brother filled the nursery with numerous pets of all varieties. At one stage, the menagerie consisted of a green frog, two lizards, some water newts, a snake and a rabbit, all of which were carefully studied by the children.

From the age of 16 Beatrix Potter took most of her summer holidays in the Lake District with her family. They often stayed on the shores of Derwentwater, a lake popular with many sportsmen, photographers and painters. Beatrix loved Derwentwater from her first visit. She climbed the fells around the lake and went out to the four little islands in the middle. She walked in the woods by the shore, watching the squirrels there, and observed the rabbits in the gardens of the houses where she stayed. She filled little notebooks with her watercolour sketches of the surrounding landscapes. The name of Beatrix Potter is forever associated with the Lake District, and her little books evoke the timeless beauty of the area to millions who have never visited it.

Rupert Potter, a keen amateur photographer, often took pictures of Derwentwater.

A happy Christmas to you.

Above, left: Beatrix observed her pet rabbits' behaviour and painted them in different positions.
Above, right: One of Beatrix's Christmas card designs, published in 1870

Noel Moore

From an early age Beatrix drew everything around her, and covered pages with sketches of animals. Her childhood sketchbooks feature fantasy pictures of animals engaged in human activities, such as rabbits ice skating and wearing clothes. With the encouragement of her Uncle Henry, who suggested that she might try selling her drawings, Beatrix began work on six whimsical designs using her pet rabbit as her model. They were bought for £6 by the publisher Hildesheimer & Faulkner, who asked to see more of her work. Beatrix was delighted. Some of the designs were published as Christmas and New Year cards in 1890. At the age of 24, Beatrix had begun her professional career. The earning of her own money was a source of great comfort to Beatrix, who had always dreamed of being independent.

Beatrix Potter enjoyed writing letters to children, and it was in these letters that she began to write and illustrate her stories. A picture letter dated 4th September 1893 (see overleaf) was the origin of *The Tale of Peter Rabbit*. The letter was sent to Noel Moore, who was the son of Beatrix's ex-governess, when he was ill in bed. It told the story of a disobedient rabbit named Peter, and it has become one of the most quoted and famous letters ever written. A few years later, it occurred to Beatrix Potter that she might make a little book out of the story. She wrote to ask if Noel had kept the letter, and if so could she borrow it? Noel *had* kept the letter, and was glad to lend it to her.

Eastwood Dunkeld
Sep 4th 93

My dear Noel,

I don't know what to write to you, so I shall tell you a story about four little rabbits whose names were—

Flopsy, Mopsy, Cottontail and Peter.

They lived with their mother in a sand bank under the root of a big fir tree.

'Now, my dears', said old Mrs Bunny 'you may go into the field or down the lane, but don't go into Mr McGregor's garden.'

Flopsy, Mopsy & Cottontail, who were good little rabbits went down the lane to gather blackberries, but Peter, who was very naughty

ran straight away to Mr McGregor's garden and squeezed underneath the gate.

First he ate some lettuce, and some broad beans, then some radishes, and then, feeling rather sick, he went to look for some parsley; but round the end of a cucumber frame whom should he meet but Mr McGregor!

Mr McGregor was planting out young cabbages but he jumped up & ran after Peter waving a rake & calling out 'Stop thief'!

Peter was most dreadfully frightened & rushed all over the garden, for he had forgotten the way back to the gate. He lost one of his shoes among the cabbages

Above and right: Beatrix Potter's picture letter to Noel Moore, sent from Scotland in 1893

and the other shoe amongst the potatoes. After losing them he ran on four legs & went faster, so that I think he would

have got away altogether, if he had not unfortunately run into a gooseberry net and got caught fast by the large buttons on his jacket. It was a blue jacket with brass buttons; quite new.

Mr McGregor came up with a basket which he intended to pop on the top of Peter, but Peter wriggled out just in time,
leaving his jacket behind,

and this time he found the gate, slipped underneath and ran home safely.

Mr McGregor hung up the little jacket & shoes for a scarecrow, to frighten the black birds.

Peter was ill during the evening, in consequence of over eating himself. His mother put him to bed and gave him a dose of camomile tea,

but Flopsy, Mopsy, and Cottontail had bread and milk and blackberries for supper.   I am coming back to London next Thursday, so I hope I shall see you soon, and the new baby.   I remain, dear Noel, yours affectionately
Beatrix Potter.

Canon Hardwicke Rawnsley

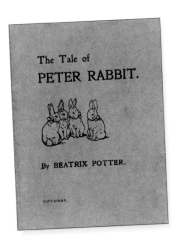

A first edition copy of The Tale of Peter Rabbit, *privately printed in 1901*

Canon Hardwicke Rawnsley, a friend of the Potter family and their local vicar in the Lake District, was the author of a popular collection of moral poems for children. With his help, the manuscript of *The Tale of Peter Rabbit* was sent to at least six publishers. Incredible though it now seems, one by one, these publishers rejected it! Undaunted, Beatrix had 250 copies of her story printed privately and those that she did not give away as presents she sold for 1/2d. Meanwhile, Beatrix and Canon Rawnsley continued to search for a commercial publisher for the book. Frederick Warne & Co. was interested in publishing the story, but strongly felt that colour illustrations were needed. Initially, Beatrix was against using colour, feeling it would be too expensive and also citing the 'rather uninteresting colour of a good many of the subjects which are most of them rabbit brown and green.' Once they persuaded Beatrix to use colour, Warne agreed to publish the story in 1902.

As in all her Tales, Beatrix used simple, direct language and never patronised her young readers. She tested out her prose on friends' children and responded to their requests. Much of the appeal of her Tales comes from their blend of light relief and serious undertones. Though most of the stories have happy endings, the characters do suffer the consequences of their actions: Peter, for instance, goes to bed with a stomach ache as a result of overindulgence in Mr. McGregor's garden. Many letters were exchanged between Beatrix and her publishers, her strong character emerging in the correspondence as the book progressed. Beatrix was interested in all aspects of book production. She had decided, informed opinions about everything from price and design, to format and the quality of the colour printing. Beatrix wanted the book to be as cheap as possible, so that children could afford to buy it with their pocket money. She was equally emphatic that the book be small, to accommodate little hands.

By the end of 1903 over 50,000 copies of *The Tale of Peter Rabbit* had been sold. 'The public must be fond of rabbits!' wrote Beatrix, 'What an appalling quantity of Peter.' *The Tale of Peter Rabbit* is as appealing today as when the story was first published, and

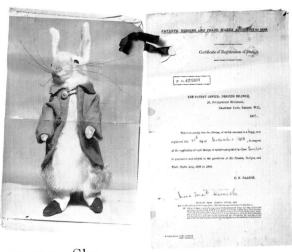

Beatrix's Peter Rabbit doll had lead shot inside its feet to make it stand upright.

Beatrix had a theory to explain its success. She wrote in 1905, 'It is much more satisfactory to address a real live child; I often think that that was the secret of the success of Peter Rabbit, it was written to a child—not made to order.' A keen businesswoman, Beatrix paid close attention to what her audience wanted and looked for ways to capitalise on her popular creations. Soon after *The Tale of Peter Rabbit* was published, she began to make a Peter Rabbit doll. 'I am cutting out calico patterns of Peter, I have not got it right yet, but the expression is going to be lovely; especially the whiskers—(pulled out of a brush!).' She registered her doll at the Patent office in London on 28th December 1903. The doll was followed the next year by wallpaper and then a Peter Rabbit board game devised by Beatrix herself.

There has been much speculation about the setting for the story, but Beatrix herself did not know for sure which Lakeland location had inspired her when she wrote the picture letter to Noel. In a letter written in 1942, she wrote, 'Peter was so composite and scattered in locality that I have found it troublesome to explain its various sources . . .' But although there is not one specific local setting for the story, the real Peter Rabbit, who was Beatrix's

A watercolour of Peter Rabbit, painted in 1899

Beatrix with Benjamin Bouncer on a lead in 1891

pet, is well known. Beatrix's rabbit, Peter Piper, lived to be eight years old and used to stretch out in front of the fire on the hearth rug like a cat. Beatrix never forgot the hero of her first little book. In one of her privately printed copies of *The Tale of Peter Rabbit* she wrote, 'In affectionate remembrance of poor old Peter Rabbit . . . whatever the limitations of his intellect or shortcomings of his fur, and his ears and toes, his disposition was uniformly amiable and his temper unfailingly sweet. An affectionate companion and a quiet friend.'

Beatrix Potter spent the summer of 1903 at Fawe Park, a large country house with a beautiful garden on the shore of Derwentwater. Soon after she arrived, she sent her editor, Norman Warne, a draft of what she called 'the rabbit story,' a sequel to *The Tale of Peter Rabbit*. Beatrix Potter modelled the hero of *The Tale of Benjamin Bunny* on her first pet rabbit, who had been smuggled into the nursery in a paper bag. His name was Benjamin H. Bouncer, or Bounce for short, and he was very fond of hot buttered toast and sweets. She described him as 'a noisy, cheerful determined animal, inclined to attack strangers'. *The Tale of Benjamin Bunny* continued the exploits of Peter Rabbit, who had wandered into Mr. McGregor's garden and very nearly ended up in a pie. Now, joined by his self-possessed cousin Benjamin, Peter sets out to recover his lost clothes from the scarecrow in the garden and has many adventures on the way.

A few weeks later, Beatrix Potter informed Norman Warne that she was making good progress with the drawings, and on 27th August she wrote, 'I have drawn a good many sketches for backgrounds of rabbits already which is perhaps as well, as the rain has come here at last.' By the end of the summer the backgrounds for *The Tale of Benjamin Bunny* were completed. Back in London Beatrix settled down for the winter months to continue working on the new book. In the middle of February 1904 Beatrix Potter wrote to Warne, 'I have nearly finished B. Bunny except the cat.'

Over the course of working together on five books, Beatrix and her editor had established a warm rapport. Though Beatrix's visits to the Frederick Warne offices were always chaperoned, the two exchanged letters nearly every day which allowed their friendship to flourish. On 25th July 1905, Norman Warne sent Beatrix a proposal of marriage, which she immediately accepted despite her parents' disapproval. At 39 years of age, Beatrix was determined to follow her heart, though she did appease her parents by keeping the engagement a secret. Unfortunately, only one month later, Norman died suddenly from a form of leukemia while Beatrix was on holiday with her family. Devastated, Beatrix took solace in her work. Earlier that summer Beatrix had used her book royalties to purchase Hill Top Farm, a working farm in the Lake District village of Near Sawrey. She drew inspiration from the tranquil surrounding landscape and set to work on her next books.

In the early months of 1909 Beatrix put the finishing touches to a new story about Peter Rabbit and Benjamin Bunny. 'I have done lots of sketches —not all to the purpose—and will now endeavour to finish up the F. Bunnies without further delay.'

Six pencil studies of Benjamin, drawn in 1890

Norman Warne

A preliminary watercolour drawing of the country gardens at Gwaynynog

Miniature letters from the Flopsy Bunnies, sent by Beatrix to a young reader

The Tale of The Flopsy Bunnies is set in the garden of her uncle's house, Gwaynynog, in Wales, a charming old house in the middle of a rambling country garden which Beatrix loved to sketch. Always at her best when painting rabbits, flowers and gardens, Beatrix used her skills to great advantage when illustrating this little book. A number of her preliminary sketches for the garden scenes have survived and they show the care she took to prepare each illustration.

It was natural for Beatrix to invite her readers to find out what had happened to the grown-up Peter Rabbit and his naughty cousin. The villain of the tale is Mr. McGregor again, but Benjamin Bunny is now married to Peter Rabbit's sister, Flopsy, and the six Flopsy Bunnies of the title are their children. Beatrix recognised that her readers enjoyed the 'independence' of her characters. She understood that they liked to imagine Benjamin and Peter 'busily absorbed in their own doings'— even marrying and having a family—long after the story was over and the book was closed. Fond of the Flopsy Bunnies, Beatrix wrote about their adventures again as part of her collection of miniature letters for the children she knew. She wrote some tiny letters which appear to come from various little Flopsy bunnies. The letters decrease in size and content according to the age and size of each little brother and sister rabbit, until those supposedly written by the tiniest bunnies are nothing more than a scribble and a few kisses.

Benjamin and Flopsy's large family, which they have great difficulty keeping track of, was the subject for another little book published in 1912. *The Tale of Mr. Tod* is about the kidnapping of the bunnies by an unpleasant badger named Tommy Brock. Tommy Brock brings the baby rabbits to the house of Mr. Tod, the fox, and very nearly eats them. Disaster is only averted when a terrific battle between Mr. Tod and his uninvited house guest distracts the two predators from the bunnies. Once again, Benjamin turns to his cousin Peter for assistance, and together they stage a daring rescue of the babies. Another of Peter's sisters, Cottontail, makes a brief appearance when she points the rescue party in the right direction.

A long, rather dark Tale featuring disagreeable principal characters, *The Tale of Mr. Tod* marked a change from writing what Beatrix described as, 'goody goody books about nice people'. Due to her preoccupation with her new farming career, Beatrix had less time for painting and therefore the majority of the book's illustrations are framed line drawings in the style of woodcuts.

Beatrix's watercolour painting of the banks of Esthwaite Water

The watercolours included, however, feature real-life landscapes of Sawrey. Bull Banks, where Mr. Tod lives in summer, was a pasture on Castle Farm, where Beatrix now lived. Mr. Tod is also depicted walking along the banks of Esthwaite Water, one of Beatrix's favourite Lakeland views.

Although Beatrix's publishers worried that the protagonists in *The Tale of Mr. Tod* were unlikeable, Beatrix knew that children enjoyed reading about misconduct. *The Story of A Fierce Bad Rabbit*, published in 1906, was written for her

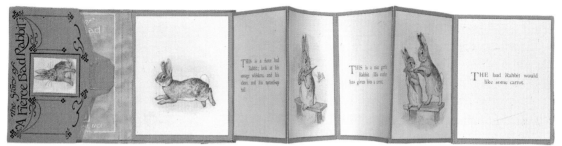

A first edition copy of The Story of A Fierce Bad Rabbit, *in panorama format*

Beatrix and William Heelis on their wedding day, 15th October 1913

editor's daughter. This little girl had complained that Peter was too good a rabbit and that she wanted a story about a *really* naughty one. Intended for very young children, this simple story was first published as a panorama, unfolding in a long strip of pictures and text from a wallet with a tuck-in flap. This format proved unpopular with booksellers, as the picture strips tended to get unrolled, and the story was reprinted in book form in 1916.

A year after the publication of *The Tale of Mr. Tod*, Beatrix married William Heelis at the age of 47. Settling permanently in the Lake District with her solicitor husband, Beatrix became increasingly engrossed in her second career as a farmer and lost interest in her writing and illustrating. Her eyes were beginning to weaken and, as she complained good-naturedly to her editor at Frederick Warne in 1918, 'Somehow when one is up to the eyes in work with real live animals it makes one despise paper-book-animals—but I mustn't say that to my publisher!' Interested in preserving traditional farming methods, Beatrix began to breed Herdwick sheep, a variety native to the Lake District. She also bought large stretches of beautiful Lakeland countryside with her book royalties. A pioneering member of the National Trust, Beatrix recognised the importance of conserving the countryside from the destruction of industry and holidaymakers. When she died in 1943, Beatrix left her land and 15 farms to the nation for future generations to enjoy.

Today, *The Tale of Peter Rabbit* has been translated into 28 languages and is published all

Peter Rabbit's Race Game, based on a 1907 design by Beatrix, was published in 1917.

over the world. Timeless classics, the books continue to sell in their millions and have been treasured by generations of children. Today Peter can be found on products ranging from baby clothes to chocolates. This merchandising began with Beatrix Potter's own interest in finding new ways to explore and expand the imaginary world she had created. Enjoying business negotiations, Beatrix was actively involved in developing what she called her 'sideshows'. Beatrix always took care to ensure that the reproduction of her characters on merchandise—whether on china tea sets, wooden figurines, dolls or painting books—was faithful to the original and retained the magic of the very first little 'rabbit book'. Towards the end of her life Beatrix Potter wrote, 'If I have done anything— even a little—to help small children on the road to enjoy and appreciate honest, simple pleasures, I have done a bit of good.' She was a remarkable woman, with a truly original imagination, artistic and literary talent, vision and the strength of mind to find creative fulfilment.

Above and below: Early Peter Rabbit merchandise

The Tale of
Peter Rabbit

1902

ONCE upon a time there
were four little Rabbits,
and their names were—

        Flopsy,
      Mopsy,
    Cotton-tail,
and Peter.

They lived with their
Mother in a sand-bank,
underneath the root of
a very big fir-tree.

"Now, my dears,"
said old Mrs. Rabbit
one morning, "you
may go into the fields or down the lane, but don't
go into Mr. McGregor's garden: your Father
had an accident there; he was put in
a pie by Mrs. McGregor.

"Now run along, and don't
get into mischief. I am going
out."

Then old Mrs. Rabbit took a basket and her umbrella, and went through the wood to the baker's. She bought a loaf of brown bread and five currant buns.

Flopsy, Mopsy, and Cotton-tail, who were good little bunnies, went down the lane to gather blackberries.

But Peter, who was very naughty, ran straight away to Mr. McGregor's garden, and squeezed under the gate!

First he ate some lettuces and some French beans; and then he ate some radishes.

And then, feeling rather sick, he went to look for some parsley.

But round the end of a cucumber frame, whom should he meet but Mr. McGregor!

Mr. McGregor was on his hands and knees planting out young cabbages, but he jumped up and ran after Peter, waving a rake and calling out, "Stop thief!"

Peter was most dreadfully frightened; he rushed all over the garden, for he had forgotten the way back to the gate.

He lost one of his shoes among the cabbages, and the other shoe amongst the potatoes.

After losing them, he ran on four legs and went faster, so that I think he might have got away altogether if he had not unfortunately run into a gooseberry net, and got caught by the large buttons on his jacket.

It was a blue jacket with brass buttons, quite new.

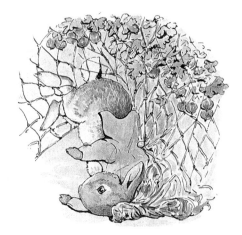

Peter gave himself up for lost, and shed big tears; but his sobs were overheard by some friendly sparrows, who flew to him in great excitement, and implored him to exert himself.

Mr. McGregor came up with a sieve, which he intended to pop upon the top of Peter; but Peter wriggled out just in time, leaving his jacket behind him.

And rushed into the tool-shed, and jumped into a can. It would have been a beautiful thing to hide in, if it had not had so much water in it.

Mr. McGregor was quite sure that Peter was somewhere in the tool-shed, perhaps hidden underneath a flower-pot. He began to turn them over carefully, looking under each.

Presently Peter sneezed—"Kertyschoo!" Mr. McGregor was after him in no time.

And tried to put his foot upon Peter, who jumped out of a window, upsetting three plants. The window was too small for Mr. McGregor, and he was tired of running after Peter. He went back to his work.

Peter sat down to rest; he was out of breath and trembling with fright, and he had not the least idea which way to go.

Also he was very damp with sitting in that can.

After a time he began to wander about, going lippity—lippity—not very fast, and looking all round.

He found a door in a wall; but it was locked, and there was no room for a fat little rabbit to squeeze underneath.

An old mouse was running in and out over the stone door-step, carrying peas and beans to her family in the wood. Peter asked her the way to the gate, but she had such a large pea in her mouth that she could not answer. She only shook her head at him. Peter began to cry.

Then he tried to find his way straight across the garden, but he became more and more puzzled. Presently, he came to a pond where Mr. McGregor filled his water-cans. A white cat was staring at some gold-fish, she sat very, very still, but now and then the tip of her tail twitched as if it were alive. Peter thought it best to go away without speaking to her; he had heard about cats from his cousin, little Benjamin Bunny.

He went back towards the tool-shed, but suddenly, quite close to him, he heard the noise of a hoe—scr-r-ritch, scratch, scratch, scritch. Peter scuttered underneath the bushes. But presently, as nothing happened, he came out, and climbed upon a wheelbarrow and peeped over. The first thing he saw was Mr. McGregor hoeing onions. His back was turned towards Peter, and beyond him was the gate!

Peter got down very quietly off the wheelbarrow, and started running as fast as he could go, along a straight walk behind some black-currant bushes.

Mr. McGregor caught sight of him at the corner, but Peter did not care. He slipped underneath the gate, and was safe at last in the wood outside the garden.

Mr. McGregor hung up the little jacket and the shoes for a scarecrow to frighten the blackbirds.

Peter never stopped running or looked behind him till he got home to the big fir-tree.

He was so tired that he flopped down upon the nice soft sand on the floor of the rabbit-hole and shut his eyes. His mother was busy cooking; she wondered what he had done with his clothes. It was the second little jacket and pair of shoes that Peter had lost in a fortnight!

I am sorry to say that Peter was not very well during the evening.

His mother put him to bed, and made some camomile tea; and she gave a dose of it to Peter!

"One table-spoonful to be taken at bed-time."

But Flopsy, Mopsy, and Cotton-tail had bread and milk and black-berries for supper.

THE END

THE TALE OF BENJAMIN BUNNY

1904

ONE morning a little rabbit sat on a bank. He pricked his ears and listened to the trit-trot, trit-trot of a pony.

A gig was coming along the road; it was driven by Mr. McGregor, and beside him sat Mrs. McGregor in her best bonnet.

As soon as they had passed, little Benjamin Bunny slid down into the road, and set off—with a hop, skip and a jump—to call upon his relations, who lived in the wood at the back of Mr. McGregor's garden.

That wood was full of rabbit holes; and in the neatest sandiest hole of all, lived Benjamin's aunt and his cousins—Flopsy, Mopsy, Cotton-tail and Peter.

Old Mrs. Rabbit was a widow; she earned her living by knitting rabbit-wool mittens and muffetees (I once bought a pair at a bazaar). She also sold herbs, and rosemary tea, and rabbit-tobacco (which is what *we* call lavender).

Little Benjamin did not very much want to see his Aunt.

He came round the back of the fir-tree, and nearly tumbled upon the top of his Cousin Peter.

Peter was sitting by himself. He looked poorly, and was dressed in a red cotton pocket-handkerchief.

"Peter,"—said little Benjamin, in a whisper—"who has got your clothes?"

Peter replied—"The scarecrow
in Mr. McGregor's garden,"
and described how he had been
chased about the garden, and
had dropped his shoes and coat.

Little Benjamin sat down
beside his cousin, and assured
him that Mr. McGregor had
gone out in a gig, and Mrs.
McGregor also; and certainly
for the day, because she was
wearing her best bonnet.

Peter said he hoped that it
would rain.

At this point, old Mrs.
Rabbit's voice was heard inside
the rabbit hole, calling—
"Cotton-tail! Cotton-tail!
Fetch some more camomile!"

Peter said he thought he
might feel better if he went
for a walk.

They went away hand in hand, and got upon the flat top of the wall at the bottom of the wood. From here they looked down into Mr. McGregor's garden. Peter's coat and shoes were plainly to be seen upon the scarecrow, topped with an old tam-o-shanter of Mr. McGregor's.

Little Benjamin said, "It spoils people's clothes to squeeze under a gate; the proper way to get in, is to climb down a pear tree."

Peter fell down head first; but it was of no consequence, as the bed below was newly raked and quite soft.

It had been sown with lettuces.

They left a great many odd little foot-marks all over the bed, especially little Benjamin, who was wearing clogs.

Little Benjamin said that the first thing to be done was to get back Peter's clothes, in order that they might be able to use the pocket-handkerchief.

They took them off the scarecrow. There had been rain during the night; there was water in the shoes, and the coat was somewhat shrunk.

Benjamin tried on the tam-o-shanter, but it was too big for him.

Then he suggested that they should fill the pocket-handkerchief with onions, as a little present for his Aunt.

Peter did not seem to be enjoying himself; he kept hearing noises.

Benjamin, on the contrary, was perfectly at home, and ate a lettuce leaf. He said that he was in the habit of coming to the garden with his father to get lettuces for their Sunday dinner.

(The name of little Benjamin's papa was old Mr. Benjamin Bunny.)

The lettuces certainly were very fine.

Peter did not eat anything; he said he should like to go home. Presently he dropped half the onions.

Little Benjamin said that it was not possible to get back up the pear-tree, with a load of vegetables. He led the way boldly towards the other end of the garden. They went along a little walk on planks, under a sunny red-brick wall.

The mice sat on their door-steps cracking cherry-stones, they winked at Peter Rabbit and little Benjamin Bunny.

Presently Peter let the
pocket-handkerchief go
again.

They got amongst
flowerpots, and frames
and tubs; Peter heard
noises worse than ever,
his eyes were as big as
lolly-pops!

He was a step or two in
front of his cousin, when
he suddenly stopped.

This is what those little rabbits saw round that corner!

Little Benjamin took one look, and then, in half a minute less than no time, he hid himself and Peter and the onions underneath a large basket . . .

The cat got up and stretched herself, and came and sniffed at the basket.

Perhaps she liked the smell of onions!

Anyway, she sat down upon the top of the basket.

She sat there for *five hours*.

*   *   *

I cannot draw you a picture
of Peter and Benjamin underneath the basket, because it
was quite dark, and because
the smell of onions was fear-
ful; it made Peter Rabbit
and little Benjamin cry.

The sun got round behind the wood, and it was quite late in
the afternoon; but still the cat sat upon the basket.

At length there was a
pitter-patter, pitter-patter,
and some bits of mortar fell
from the wall above.

The cat looked up and saw
old Mr. Benjamin Bunny
prancing along the top of the
wall of the upper terrace.

He was smoking a pipe of
rabbit-tobacco, and had a
little switch in his hand.

He was looking for his son.

Old Mr. Bunny had no opinion whatever of cats.

He took a tremendous jump off the top of the wall on to the top of the cat, and cuffed it off the basket, and kicked it into the green-house, scratching off a handful of fur. The cat was too much surprised to scratch back.

When old Mr. Bunny had driven the cat into the green-house, he locked the door.

Then he came back to the basket and took out his son Benjamin by the ears, and whipped him with the little switch.

Then he took out his nephew Peter.

Then he took out the handkerchief of onions, and marched out of the garden.

When Mr. McGregor returned about half an hour later, he observed several things which perplexed him.

It looked as though some person had been walking all over the garden in a pair of clogs—only the foot-marks were too ridiculously little!

Also he could not understand how the cat could have managed to shut herself up *inside* the green-house, locking the door upon the *outside*.

When Peter got home, his mother forgave him, because she was so glad to see that he had found his shoes and coat. Cotton-tail and Peter folded up the pocket-handkerchief, and old Mrs. Rabbit strung up the onions and hung them from the kitchen ceiling, with the bunches of herbs and the rabbit-tobacco.

THE END

THE TALE OF
THE
FLOPSY BUNNIES

1909

IT is said that the effect of eating too much lettuce is "soporific".

I have never felt sleepy after eating lettuces; but then *I* am not a rabbit.

They certainly had a very soporific effect upon the Flopsy Bunnies!

When Benjamin Bunny grew up, he married his Cousin Flopsy. They had a large family, and they were very improvident and cheerful.

I do not remember the separate names of their children; they were generally called the "Flopsy Bunnies".

As there was not always quite enough to eat—Benjamin used to borrow cabbages from Flopsy's brother, Peter Rabbit, who kept a nursery garden.

Sometimes Peter Rabbit had no cabbages to spare.

When this happened, the Flopsy Bunnies went across the field to a rubbish heap, in the ditch outside Mr. McGregor's garden.

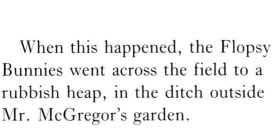

Mr. McGregor's rubbish heap was a mixture. There were jam pots and paper bags, and mountains of chopped grass from the mowing machine (which always tasted oily), and some rotten vegetable marrows and an old boot or two. One day—oh joy!—there were a quantity of overgrown lettuces, which had "shot" into flower.

The Flopsy Bunnies simply stuffed lettuces. By degrees, one after another, they were overcome with slumber, and lay down in the mown grass.

Benjamin was not so much overcome as his children. Before going to sleep he was sufficiently wide awake to put a paper bag over his head to keep off the flies.

The little Flopsy Bunnies slept delightfully in the warm sun. From the lawn beyond the garden came the distant clacketty sound of the mowing machine. The blue-bottles buzzed about the wall, and a little old mouse picked over the rubbish among the jam pots.

(I can tell you her name, she was called Thomasina Tittlemouse, a woodmouse with a long tail.)

She rustled across the paper bag, and awakened Benjamin Bunny.

The mouse apologized profusely, and said that she knew Peter Rabbit.

While she and Benjamin were talking, close under the wall, they heard a heavy tread above their heads; and suddenly Mr. McGregor emptied out a sackful of lawn mowings right upon the top of the sleeping Flopsy Bunnies! Benjamin shrank down under his paper bag. The mouse hid in a jam pot.

The little rabbits smiled sweetly in their sleep under the shower of grass; they did not awake because the lettuces had been so soporific.

They dreamt that their mother Flopsy was tucking them up in a hay bed.

Mr. McGregor looked down after emptying his sack. He saw some funny little brown tips of ears sticking up through the lawn mowings. He stared at them for some time.

Presently a fly settled on one of them and it moved.

Mr. McGregor climbed down on to the rubbish heap—

"One, two, three, four! five! six leetle rabbits!" said he as he dropped them into his sack.